For Connor and Keegan
whose great-great-grandfather helped to build
the CCC camps that opened a new world
for thousands of young men.
—Gloria

For the young men in the CCC
whose names and stories are unknown.
And for my family, may my paintings remind you
of our memories on Lake Michigan.
—Kirbi

SLEEPING BEAR PRESS™

2395 South Huron Parkway, Suite 200
Ann Arbor, MI 48104
www.sleepingbearpress.com
© Sleeping Bear Press

Printed and bound in the United States.
10 9 8 7 6 5 4 3 2 1

Library of Congress Cataloging-in-Publication Data
Names: Whelan, Gloria, author. | Fagan, Kirbi, illustrator.
Title: Summer of the tree army : a Civilian Conservation Corps story /
written by Gloria Whelan ; illustrated by Kirbi Fagan.
Description: Ann Arbor, Michigan : Sleeping Bear Press, [2021] |
Series: Tales of young Americans | Audience: Ages 6-10. | Summary:
"In Depression-era northern Michigan, a young boy meets a teenager serving
in the Civilian Conservation Corps, the work relief program established
by President Franklin D. Roosevelt to employ millions of young men
during the Great Depression"— Provided by publisher.
Identifiers: LCCN 2020031507 | ISBN 9781585363858 (hardcover)
Subjects: LCSH: Civilian Conservation Corps (U.S.)—Juvenile fiction. |
CYAC: Civilian Conservation Corps (U.S.)—Fiction. | Forest fires—Fiction. |
Depressions—1929—Fiction. | Michigan—History—20th century—Fiction.
Classification: LCC PZ7.W5718 St 2021 | DDC [E]—dc23
LC record available at https://lccn.loc.gov/2020031507

Charlie Brightelot spent his summer days exploring the woods around his home in northern Michigan, but in all his nine years, he had never seen anything like those mysterious buildings.

At dinner he asked his father, "What are they building in the woods?"

"Those are barracks. President Roosevelt got the idea of shipping fellows with no jobs up here from the city. They call them the Civilian Conservation Corps—CCC for short."

"There's a depression right now, Charlie," his mother said. "Those young men are having a hard time making a living."

"Well, they don't have to be running around in our woods," Mr. Brightelot said. "From what I hear, all they do is eat three meals a day, sleep, and sit around."

It was June and school was out. Charlie forgot about the barracks. Each day, after he had finished feeding the chickens, milking the goat, and weeding the vegetable garden, he was out in the woods.

It wasn't until August when Charlie peeked through the trees and saw a group of young men. They were on a truck full of small trees.

Charlie followed the truck through the woods to a place where there had been a forest fire. Dead trees rose like skeletons. Charlie watched as the men planted a tiny tree near each dead one.

On his way home, Charlie was picking wild raspberries when he heard someone cry out for help. Thrashing through the bushes was an older boy wearing the CCC uniform. He was skinny and looked like he might be in high school.

When the boy saw Charlie, he shouted, "Something's after me!"

Charlie saw the way the grass
was tramped down and that some
of the berry bushes were crushed.

"It's just a bear," he said. "Probably more afraid of you than you are
of him. How come you're out here in the woods by yourself?"

"We were planting trees and I got separated from the others. The more I looked for them, the more lost I got. My name's Luke."

"Hi, I'm Charlie. I'll show you the way back to your camp," Charlie said. "Help yourself to the berries. They're free. And maybe sometime I could show you a little lake where I fish. We can catch as many perch as we can eat."

"Really? That would be great. We get Sundays off," Luke said.

Charlie said, "I'll come next week and get you."

On Sunday Luke was waiting for him.
The other CCC men were in groups talking
or playing cards. A couple of them were
strumming on banjos.

Luke told Charlie, "I've got a brother about your age at home.
I really miss him."

"You can tell him how you met me in the woods," Charlie said.
"Now we need to find some worms."

When the boys arrived at the Brightelots, Mr. Brightelot grumbled. "I don't know what you CCC fellows are doing up here while our taxes are paying for your keep."

Luke said, "We work hard, sir. We've planted thousands of trees and we repaired that old bridge over the river."

Mrs. Brightelot welcomed Luke. "You're skin and bones, young man. Go ahead and eat up."

Luke needed no coaxing. "There's plenty of food at the camp, but none as good as this."

The next morning Charlie's father woke him up. Charlie could smell smoke. Out the window the sky was orange.

His father said, "Get up. There's a forest fire and it's nearby."

As they went outside, they saw the CCC trucks rushing by. They were on their way to fight the fire.

Mr. Brightelot got into his truck. "Those city boys are going to need all the help they can get."

"I'm going with you," Charlie said.

"You're too young, son. You'll only be in the way."

But when his father wasn't looking,
Charlie jumped into the bed of the truck.

As they neared the fire, Charlie could feel its scorching heat. He began to wish he had stayed home. The truck lurched to a sudden stop and he hopped out.

His father was angry. "You shouldn't have disobeyed me. But since you're here, you may as well make yourself useful." He pointed to a pail and a dipper. "You can give drinking water to the men fighting the fire."

Heavy smoke gave the sky the darkness of a violent thunderstorm.
Silhouetted against the glow of the flames, a crew of CCC men
was digging a trench.

Mr. Brightelot explained to Charlie, "They're digging that trench to clear the soil of brush and grass and anything else that might burn. With nothing to feed it, they hope when the fire gets there, it will stop. I have to admit that's smart thinking."

By afternoon the dancing red colors had disappeared, leaving a smoky, smudged sky. It was nearly evening when the CCC trucks finally rumbled away. As Luke went by, he called out to Charlie, who waved back. His dad waved, too.

Mr. Brightelot said, "Those CCC boys earned their keep. The folks around here

That Sunday Charlie and his father took
Luke to their secret fishing spot. Minutes after
Luke had tossed in his line, he hooked a bass
as big as a cat. Charlie and his father cheered
him on. Mr. Brightelot took a picture of
Luke holding the big fish.

"You can send that to your mom and dad," he said.
"Tell them you did a great job up here."

"I'll tell them this has been my best summer," Luke said.

A NOTE FROM *the* AUTHOR

It was the Great Depression. One out of every four workers was without a job. President Roosevelt passed the Emergency Conservation Work Act, creating opportunities for unemployed young men to do conservation work on federal and state land. In 1933 Michigan opened its first Civilian Conservation Corps (CCC) camp near Sault Ste. Marie.

The young men had to be single males between the ages of 17 and 23, unemployed, US citizens, and not attending school. The men were paid 30 dollars a month, 22 to 25 of which was sent to their families. One hundred thousand of these young men with little or no schooling were taught to read and write. The camps prepared the men for employment, teaching discipline and good work skills. Black and White young men worked side by side until 1935, when there was a ruling by President Roosevelt that all CCC camps be segregated, egregiously denying deserved equal opportunities for Black men.

According to Roger L. Rosentreter's "Roosevelt's Tree Army: Michigan's Civilian Conservation Corps," Michigan had around 57 camps and 102,814 CCC participants. The CCC men planted 484 million trees, stocked 156 million fish, fought forest fires, and constructed 7,000 miles of truck trails, 504 bridges, and 222 buildings.

At the CCC museum near the city of Roscommon, Michigan, there is a replica of a CCC barracks as well as displays of uniforms, firefighting equipment, and pictures of the men who worked at the camp. I would also like to acknowledge the help of Hillary Pine, historian with the Michigan Department of Natural Resources.

The CCC camps played an important part in my own life. As a child I stayed with my parents for a summer in a cabin in northern Michigan, where my father was working on the construction of one of the camps.